Worse Things Happen at Sea!

BOOK 3

McTavish Charts & Maps
For the transfer of serious impressions

Cheezilla!

OXFORD

Also by Alan Snow

WORSE THINGS
HAPPEN AT SEA!

HERE BE MONSTERS!

CHEEZILLA!

WORSE THINGS HAPPEN AT SEA!

A TALE OF
PIRATES, POISON, AND MONSTERS

by Alan Snow

OXFORD

To Issy, whose father is not very good at drawing horses
& Theo, Maya, Finn, Tom and Ruby

OXFORD
UNIVERSITY PRESS

Great Clarendon Street, Oxford OX2 6DP
Oxford University Press is a department of the University of Oxford.
It furthers the University's objective of excellence in research, scholarship,
and education by publishing worldwide in

Oxford New York

Auckland Cape Town Dar es Salaam Hong Kong Karachi
Kuala Lumpur Madrid Melbourne Mexico City Nairobi
New Delhi Shanghai Taipei Toronto

With offices in

Argentina Austria Brazil Chile Czech Republic France Greece
Guatemala Hungary Italy Japan Poland Portugal Singapore
South Korea Switzerland Thailand Turkey Ukraine Vietnam

Oxford is a registered trade mark of Oxford University Press
in the UK and in certain other countries

© Alan Snow 2011

The moral rights of the author have been asserted

Database right Oxford University Press (maker)

First published in 2010 as part of Worse Things Happen At Sea!
First published in this edition 2011

British Library Cataloguing in Publication Data

Data available

ISBN: 978-0-19-279274-7
1 3 5 7 9 10 8 6 4 2

Printed in Great Britain

Paper used in the production of this book is a natural,
recyclable product made from wood grown in sustainable forests.
The manufacturing process conforms to the environmental
regulations of the country of origin.

CONTENTS

Johnson's Taxonomy
of Trolls and Creatures

Albatross
A true sea bird that has been known to spend up to 10 years without ever visiting land. Has large wingspan (3.5 metres). Can live up to 85 years and pairs for life.

Cabbage Island
A legendary island that is supposed to be in the southern Pacific. Said to be the home of strange plants with incredible powers. While it is not known if this island exists it is mentioned in many travelogues of the region and turns up in folklore surrounding cheese and health.

Crow
The crow is an intelligent bird, capable of living in many environments. Usually they are charming company, but should be kept from providing the entertainment. Failure to do so may result in tedium, for while intelligent, crows seem to lack taste in the choice of music, and conversational topics.

Boxtrolls
A sub-species of the common troll, they are very shy, so live inside a box. These they gather from the backs of large shops. They are somewhat troublesome creatures—as they have a passion for everything mechanical and no understanding of the concept of ownership (they steal anything which is not bolted down and, more often than not, anything which is). It is very dangerous to leave tools lying about where they might find them.

Cheese
Wild English Cheeses live in bogs. This is unlike their French cousins who live in caves. They are nervous beasties, that eat grass by night, in the meadows and woodlands. They are also of very low intelligence, and are panicked by almost anything that catches them unawares. Cheese make easy quarry for hunters, being rather easier to catch than a dead sheep.

Guillemot (paid entry)
Famously the name of the founder of the fabulous south sea trading company and mail order business. Providers of exotic and budget items for every home. Send a stamped addressed envelope and you will be amazed at just how quickly we respond (3 year delivery guaranteed).

The Members
Members of the secretive Ratbridge Cheese Guild, that was thought to have died out after the 'Great Cheese Crash'. It was an evil organization that rigged the cheese market, and doctored and adulterated lactose-based food stuffs.

Legendary Monsters
Often found wandering the southern sea and should be avoided at all cost, unless you are the owner of a Guillemot Monster-repelling Kit. These are available by mail order (see entry for Guillemot). These monsters are known to reside on many islands and thought to be the last remaining dinosaurs on the planet. Last confirmed sighting—Tokyo 1723.

Grandfather (William)
Arthur's guardian and carer. Grandfather lived underground for many years in a cave home where he pursued his interests in engineering. But after some rather unusual events both Arthur and his grandfather found themselves with a new home in the former petshop now rented by Willbury Nibble and shared with boxtrolls and Titus the cabbagehead. He now wakes up late, then spends his days in the company of Willbury and all their new friends, and has been known to sneak off on his own to the Nag's Head tavern for a crafty pint and bag of pork scratchings with a pickled egg. Now relieved of the sole care of Arthur, his favourite pastime is reading in bed with his own bucket of cocoa.

Shopping Birds
A once common bird that has now become rare due to its blatant consumerism and lack of intelligence.

Rats
Rats are known to be some of the most intelligent of all rodents, and to be considerably more intelligent than many humans. They are known to have a passion for travel, and be extremely adaptable. They often live in a symbiotic relationship with humans.

Trotting Badgers
Trotting badgers are some of the nastiest creatures to be found anywhere. With their foul temper, rapid speed, and razor-sharp teeth, it cannot be stressed just how unpleasant and dangerous these creatures are. It is only their disgusting stench that gives warning of their proximity, and when smelt it is often too late.

The Story So Far ...

DIRTY WASHING

Arthur and his grandfather are on deck of the Ratbridge Nautical Laundry, helping their rat and pirate friends pack up piles of washing. Suddenly there is a commotion—policemen and an angry mob are heading straight for them. Earlier that day, a famous countess was insulted to see underwear flying from the rigging. She wants compensation and the town is suing for damages. Everyone on the *Nautical Laundry* is arrested and ordered to appear in court the next morning.

Policemen and an angry mob

NO WAY OUT?

Now under police guard, Arthur, Grandfather, Marjorie the inventor and the rest of the crew are stuck on the ship. Grandfather knows that they must get to their friend, Willbury Nibble, a retired lawyer, who can help. Marjorie suggests using the

She pushed up the periscope and looked about

old submarine at the side of the ship. They escape, but a collision in the canal leaves Grandfather injured.

IN THE DOCK

The next day, Willbury does his best to defend the crew—but a huge fine of ten thousand groats is imposed upon the *Nautical Laundry*. How on earth will they find that sum of money?

Stuffed into the dock was the entire crew

BLACK JOLLOP!

'IT WORKS! It really works!'

Meanwhile, a mysterious doctor has opened a new health spa. Ratbridge residents are clamouring for a free dose of miracle medicine 'Black Jollop', said to cure all ills. Arthur takes Grandfather into the spa to be cured. Later, they receive some alarming news: supplies of Black Jollop are low. The doctor offers the crew of the *Nautical Laundry* ten thousand groats to undertake a journey to collect the secret ingredient.

PREPARATIONS

Arthur is devastated when he is told that he cannot go on the journey. Marjorie entrusts him with the key of the submarine. Seeing how unhappy Arthur is, Grandfather changes his mind and allows Arthur to go— but when they reach the towpath, the ship has already gone! Remembering the key to the submarine, Arthur and Fish, the boxtroll, clamber into it and together they head off down the canal in pursuit.

Arthur turned and walked away down the towpath.

SURPRISE!

That evening, Arthur and Fish sneak on to the ship when it docks for the night, and stow away in an old barrel. But the next day, when the ship reaches international waters, the horrid truth emerges—the doctor has tricked them all into coming aboard ship with the villainous Archibald Snatcher and his men!

'Surprise!'

DISASTER!

From the barrel, Arthur and Fish watch in horror as Snatcher seizes control of the ship and appoints his own men as the crew. No one can work out why he would want to journey so far for Black Jollop's secret ingredient—or what he intends to do with it. Arthur watches as his friends are forced to slave for Snatcher and make do with only horrid hardtack to eat.

Arthur peering out of barrel

GOO!

In a moment of mischief, and as payback for measly rations, Bert tells Snatcher of a 'tradition' which involves daubing crew members with foul-smelling goo. While Snatcher dresses as

Bert and the goo

Neptune for the ceremony, Bert stirs a stinking mixture of glue, oil, bilge water, treacle and trotting badgers' droppings. With the exception of Fingle, who escapes up the rigging, none of Snatcher's men are safe from the smelly concoction.

TROTTING BADGERS

Later that evening, Arthur and Fish sneak out of their hiding place and manage to trap Snatcher, his crew, and the doctor below decks by using the vicious trotting badgers Snatcher brought aboard. With the villains safely out of the way, the rightful crew takes back control of the ship.

trotting badgers

CRUEL AND UNUSUAL PUNISHMENT

With the artful use of a bacon sandwich, Willbury coaxes the truth from Fingle about the real reason behind the expedition for Black Jollop. It turns out that the medicine has a terrible side effect—it brings about a mad (and illegal) craving for cheese! Now the wild cheeses of Ratbridge are under threat, for most of the town is infected ... including Grandfather!

Willbury & Fingle

CHEESY DESIRE

Snatcher's evil plans are now clear. He wants cheese eating to be legalized again! And with the demand for cheese in Ratbridge now out of control, it should be easy. All seems hopeless until Marjorie notices that the doctor is trying to signal a message: there is an antidote to the poisonous cheese lust on the very island that they are heading for!

LAND HO!

Soon a speck of lush, leafy land is visible ... Black Cabbage Island is in sight! But as the *Nautical Laundry* draws closer, a terrifying monster lurches out of the trees and into the sea ... straight for the ship! Suddenly Arthur and his friends (and enemies) are swimming for their lives ... but who will survive? And who, or what awaits them on the island?

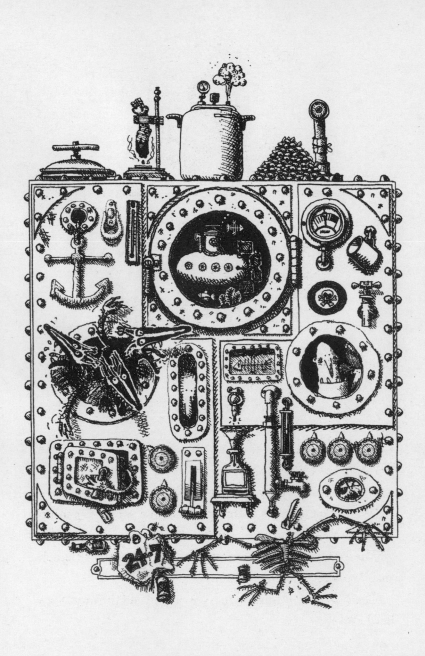

Inside the brain of the monster there was confusion

Chapter 1

MONSTROUS THOUGHTS

Inside the brain of the monster there was confusion.

'What are we going to do now?'

'Tell the neck to turn from side to side, and have the eyes look about and report back.'

'They have all jumped in the sea and are swimming for the beach,' came the message from the eyes.

'I think we've really scared them.'

'We'll have to pick them up out of the water. Open up the mouth and bend over a little bit.'

The escaping swimmers were within easy reach of a quick snap and were starting to panic.

There was a certain amount of worry inside the monster's head as well.

'If we don't start grabbing them out of the water we are going to lose some of them. Bend over more!'

'OK, jaws, when you are in position start swallowing, and try not to take in too much water.'

Arthur watched in horror as the monster struck. Its mouth lowered over three trailing swimmers and closed.

'Push Willbury faster or it will get us!'

The monster tipped its head back and swallowed. Then leant forward again for another mouthful.

The monster tipped its head back and swallowed

In the stomach the first of the screaming swimmers arrived.

'Aaaaaargh!'

Then they hit the stomach floor.

Boing! Boing! Boing!

'Uh?'

'What's going on?'

'I can't see anything.'

'Are we dead?'

'No. I don't think so. In fact I feel all right apart from being eaten by a monster.'

'Me too. Did you bounce?'

'Yes.'

'Me too.'

'What happens now?'

'I don't think it's so good. We get digested. Something like that. I should've listened more at school.'

'I should've listened more at school'

Then they covered their heads as they heard more screaming from above and a few moments later they were joined by the next mouthful.

Arthur could not bear to look back. They could hear the monster behind them and this gave the spur to swim as hard as they could. Slowly the screaming behind them grew less as more and more swimmers were swallowed, until Arthur guessed they were the last.

'Faster! We're almost at the beach.'

'Whatever happens, I just want you to know you've all been good friends to me,' Kipper spluttered.

A shadow fell over them and Arthur felt something lifting them from the water.

'GOODBYE, ARTHUR!' shouted Willbury, just before the monster's jaws closed around them all.

'GOODBYE, ARTHUR!'

1 GROAT

THE ·Ratbridge·Gazette·

BANGED TO RIGHTS

In a raid on the Ratbridge Women's Guild this afternoon twenty-seven women were arrested. Cheese hounds led the police to a church hall where the women were found in possession of shards of cheese. None of the 'Cheesy Crimesses' denied it, instead claiming not to have been able to control themselves. Do we believe this? NO! Send them down!

'Whoever has got his knee in my ear, will you kindly shift it!'

Chapter 2

GUTTED!

'Well done, jaws. I think we've got the lot of them.'

'Back to the beach?'

'I think we better had. Our stomach is so full I think we might not be able to eat for a week.'

There was some laughing inside the head and the creature made for the beach.

'Whoever has got his knee in my ear, will you kindly shift it!' demanded Kipper.

'And whoever's sitting on my head will you please shift your butt!' This time Arthur recognized Snatcher's voice from immediately below him.

'Sorry.' Arthur moved himself to cause less moaning. Then the stomach start to shake and quiver.

'We're moving!'

The creature walked slowly across the lagoon and up the beach.

A message went out from the eyes. 'OK. We are on dry land!'

On receiving this information a command went out from the head to the legs to stop.

The feet of the monster settled in the sand and the creature came to rest.

Inside the stomach the monster's breakfast fell silent. Arthur's face was pressed against a warm rubbery wall. He heard something through it. At first he wasn't sure what it was, but slowly he realized it was muffled talking.

The wall moved just above his head, pushing against him, and then a hole appeared. Daylight rushed in and a split zipped down past him.

Arthur found himself falling along with the rest of the stomach's contents on to the beach. It took a few moments before his eyes became used to the sunlight, then he heard something he didn't quite believe.

'Sorry about that. We didn't mean to scare you. But once we had, the quickest way to stop anybody drowning was to eat you.'

Surrounding them were about a hundred rather large and very apologetic looking people. They all had soft brown skin, and wore brightly coloured wraps of cloth.

A big woman walked forward towards the pile of bodies.

Arthur found himself falling, along with the rest the stomach's contents, on to the beach

'We're very sorry, but we usually spot any ships before they arrive and can scare them away.'

Arthur looked from the woman to the monster behind them. He wasn't quite sure what to expect but it didn't look so scary now. In fact it didn't look scary at all. More like a lot of scaffolding wrapped in old dirty sheets.

'It's not real!' Arthur exclaimed.

'That's right.'

'Did you make it?'

The large woman smiled. 'Yes . . . well I say yes, our people made it a couple of hundred years ago when the ships started to arrive and cause trouble. We just keep it going to stop outsiders bothering us. Worked pretty well up until now.'

'You're speaking English!' exclaimed Marjorie.

This had not struck Arthur until this point, but now it did seem odd.

'Yes. Let me explain, but first I would like to formally introduce myself and welcome you to our island. I'm Queen Florence but you can all call me Flo.'

She bowed and the contents of the monster's stomach struggled to their feet to return the greeting.

Then the queen went on. 'We hoped you might be English as we find the language so poetic. We learnt it from a sailor who got washed up here. Quite often when we have a day off we will practise it.'

'You seem to speak excellent English, ma'am,' said Willbury.

'Thank you. I try to learn as many languages as I can. It really helps to understand the cultures. What languages do you speak?'

There was an embarrassed silence from the English speakers in front of her.

'Oh well. You should try it. Our own language is very beautiful for doing maths and sciences but doesn't have so many fancy words for art and romance. Now I have a question. Why have you come here?'

There was a silence while the shipmates looked at each other rather awkwardly.

'Thank you for your welcome.' Willbury took the lead, as no one else seemed to want to. 'It's a long story but it can be put down to some of us wanting to cure some people, while others here want to poison them.'

'And which of you are which?'

The crew separated themselves from Snatcher and his mob, leaving the doctor and Fingle standing between them. Then, seeing the look on Snatcher's face, both Fingle and the doctor moved to join the crew.

Willbury pointed at Snatcher's group. 'These characters have poisoned some of our townsfolk with a potion that drives them crazy with a desire for cheese. We believe they got the ingredient from a plant from this island and that in order to cure our people we need to get another plant that grows here.'

Queen Flo looked very concerned. 'I think I know what you're talking about. The Black Cabbage Tree and the Un-cabbage Flower. But how did this happen? I didn't know anybody had taken any Cabbage Tree seeds away.'

A man standing next to the queen broke in. 'I bet it's Guillemot, and the mob from Shopping Island. You just can't trust them.'

Guillemot

There was much nodding of heads and muttering from the islanders.

'Who're they?' asked Willbury.

The man standing by the queen's side spoke again. 'There is an island five miles north of here where a people very unlike us live. It's very strange but they live to shop. We try not to have much to do with them but on occasion they do turn up. They're a right bunch!'

'Yes,' added the queen. 'On this island things are pretty perfect. We've everything we need to live on, and plenty of spare time to play and think. On their island they have everything they need too, but spend most of their time trying to outdo each other, by selling or shopping. It's very sad.'

'And this man Guillemot?'

'Guillemot is a trader. He turned up on their island and fitted right in. Ships visit their island occasionally and he organizes trading between the islanders and the ships.'

'And the ships never visit here because of your monster?'

'That's right.'

'Does your monster keep the islander from the other island away as well?

'Not really. They knew about us building the monster and don't say anything because I think it suits them that people visit them instead of us.'

'And you've met this Guillemot?'

'Yes. He's been over here a few times trying to get us to

trade with him but we're not interested. Last time he was over he came when some others needed our medicine and he charged them for a ride in his boat. So Guillemot probably knows about our seeds. I'm guessing he must have stolen some, and is in part responsible for your Cabbage Tree poisoning.'

Willbury looked at Snatcher, who was looking very ill at ease. 'Is that so?'

Willbury looked at Snatcher, who was looking very ill at ease

Snatcher smirked.

'I'll take that as a yes then.' Willbury looked back at the Queen. 'Do you think you can help us?'

'Certainly! If your people have been poisoned by our Black Cabbage Tree, it is down to us to help put things right. It may take a few nights to collect the Un-Cabbage Flowers but then you will be able to cure the mania.'

'Thank you,' said Arthur. 'My grandfather is going to need some.'

'You mean to say that they've been poisoning old people?' Queen Flo was outraged and stared at Snatcher in disbelief. The crowd around her started to look very angry.

'Yes he has. He got everybody he could to take his poison, and he wanted to come here to get more seeds so he could poison more,' said Arthur.

'And how many people in total has he poisoned?'

'It must be at least several hundred.'

'Shocking! We'll start collecting this tonight. The only time you can pick the Un-Cabbage Flowers is at night after the cabbage rain.'

Arthur and his friends looked very puzzled.

'Every evening there is a rain that falls in the forest and this washes the poison down from the Black Cabbage Trees. When this happens the Un-Cabbage Flowers start to produce the antidote and by morning the forest is safe again. If you need to make medicine to cure illnesses you need to collect Black Cabbage Tree seeds by day and then very carefully collect the Un-Cabbage Flowers by night. As we only need the Un-Cabbage Flowers we'll have to work at night. Now tell me about this horrid man,' she said, and pointed to Snatcher.

Between Arthur and the others they told the story. As soon as they had heard what had happened, the islanders offered to keep Snatcher and his men in a cave nearby.

'It's safe and they won't be able to get out. We used to use it to keep anybody who had the cheese mania before we discovered how to cure them with the Un-Cabbage Flowers.'

'So some of your people got poisoned?' asked Arthur.

'Yes. Occasionally somebody would get caught in the rain and end up having to be locked away.

'It was very sad. The cheeses who live in the forest here have no natural predators and are the only creatures not affected by the cabbage rain, but once a few people got the mania they were almost wiped out.'

The cheeses who live in the forest

If someone had been very carefully watching Snatcher at that moment, they would've seen him lick his lips and mutter to himself.

Willbury spoke. 'It would be a real blessing if you could help us. There are a few other things we need like food, fuel and fresh water, for the journey home.'

'No problem. And you're welcome to stay on the island while we get everything you need.'

'That's very kind of you.'

'Do you need to get anything from your boat?'

'Well we need to bring our water barrels ashore to fill . . .'

'Would you like to use our fishing boats, or you could use our monster?'

Willbury looked slightly panicked and spoke hurriedly. 'I think the fishing boats, if we may.'

Arthur was very disappointed by this. The chance to ride in the monster seemed very appealing.

'Boats it is then. If some of you would like to get on with that, our children can help the other members of your crew find water and food.'

The island children all nodded.

'And,' added the queen, 'would you all like to feast with us tonight before we collect Un-Cabbage Flowers?' Then she added, 'Apart from the poisoners, that is.'

Tom shot a triumphant look at Snatcher and stepped forward to speak. 'I think I can say on behalf of the non-poisoners that we would like to accept your offer of a feast.'

Everybody apart from Snatcher and his mob cheered.

'So shall we say a feast at about ten and afterward we shall start collecting Un-Cabbage Flowers?'

'YES!' came the cry.

The meeting broke up. Bert and some of the islanders set off to the cave with Snatcher and company, Kipper took a boat back to the ship with some fishermen to collect water barrels, Arthur and the other crew went off to collect food and wood with the children. The other islanders set about preparing for the feast.

Fish kept close to Arthur as they wandered into the trees. He kept looking up worriedly.

Fish kept close to Arthur

'You don't need to worry,' said a small girl. 'The Black Cabbage Trees don't start until much higher up the hill and it never rains until exactly ten o'clock. Down here are just bread fruit, bananas, coconuts and yams.'

This made Fish feel much happier. He didn't like the idea of cabbage rain one bit.

Over the next few hours a huge pile of food built up on the sands and Kipper returned in a fishing boat towing the empty water barrels behind it. The bigger pirates then took the barrels to a nearby waterfall that the children showed them and filled them up, before rolling them back to the beach.

Rolling the barrels back to the beach

When the queen saw how fast everything was being done she told them not to rush too much as it would take at least three days to collect the flowers they needed.

'This is an island. And you have to learn to move at our speed!' she joked.

This seemed very agreeable to everyone, and they decided they'd done enough and had a long swim in the waterfall pool. Fish was the first to dive in, followed by Arthur. As they swam under the base of the waterfall Fish was as happy as Arthur had ever seen him.

A long swim in the waterfall pool

NOGENS SENTENTIA PRO IGNARUS

1 GROAT

THE ·Ratbridge·Gazette·

Mass Arrests As Net Closes on 'Cheesy Crims'

Ratbridge gaol is now overflowing with 'Cheesy Crims' after a police operation last night. Retained cheese-hounds led police to over a hundred addresses and at most of these, traces of cheese were found. In total over 200 'Cheesy Crims' were apprehended.

Police stated that there could only be a few of the mob at large, and it is only a matter of days before cheese would be safe again.

Conditions inside the gaol are said to be terrible. This paper says 'SERVES THEM RIGHT'!

'Get yer vests off and start unravelling them'

Chapter 3

IN A HOLE

Snatcher seemed in a surprisingly good mood for a trapped man. Although the cave had not been used for many years, a certain number of 'things' had fallen into it and were piled up on the floor. He waited until the voices above had died away and then spoke.

'Things ain't going to end this way. I've got a plan. Gristle, collect up all these bones and bits of old stick. We are going to make a ladder.'

'How's we going to stick them together?'

Snatcher looked at his men. 'Get yer vests off and start unravelling them.'

Ratbridge had always been home to the string vest, and this garment was to be their saviour. But it was not without a cost—for what Snatcher hadn't quite banked on was the smell. Even the dowsing and swim in the sea hadn't done much to ease the personal odour of his mob.

But there was no way round it so, pinching his nose, Snatcher oversaw the construction of the ladder. The stench was almost overpowering, and by the time the ladder was ready he had nearly passed out.

'Right. Put it up against the wall.'

The ladder was six feet short of the surface.

'I think we need to build it up a bit,' suggested Gristle.

'I guess we do. Gristle and the rest of you louts, lie down!'

They lay down in a heap, and Snatcher repositioned the ladder. On top of the heap.

'Very good, lads. Keep still while I climb up.'

The sounds of pain echoed around the cave as Snatcher clambered up the heap and started up the ladder. Soon he reached the surface and looked back.

'Gristle, you next. And bring any spare string.'

Gristle pulled himself out from the pile and did as he was told. Then one by one, the person at the top of the pile lifted the ladder off themselves, and placed it back on the pile so they could then climb up. The pile grew shorter and shorter, and the ladder sunk lower and lower. The last few took some hoisting with string to get them up to the top.

'I think I'm broken,' Gristle moaned.

'Which bit of you?'

'All of me.'

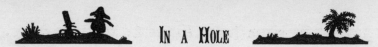
'Shut up and follow me,' snapped Snatcher. 'With luck we're going to take a monster for a walk.'

'What do you mean?'

'We're going to visit my old trading partner Guillemot, and we are going to use that monster to get there.'

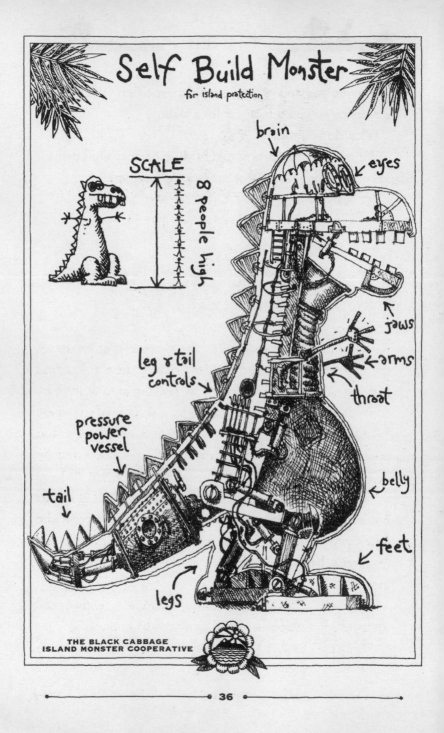

Self Build Monster
for island protection

brain

eyes

SCALE

8 people high

jaws

arms

throat

leg & tail controls

belly

pressure power vessel

tail

feet

legs

**THE BLACK CABBAGE
ISLAND MONSTER COOPERATIVE**

Shadowy figures rushed across the beach and up the tail of the monster

Chapter 4

'WALKIES!'

Arthur and his friends sat beneath the palms as guests of the Queen and the other islanders. Before them a feast was laid out and soon everybody was tucking into stone-pit-cooked pork, coconut milk cocktails and some of the finest food that Arthur had ever tasted. Everyone felt happy and optimistic—it looked as if their mission would soon be accomplished.

So engrossed were the party in their feast that they did not notice the shadowy figures rushing quietly across the beach and up the tail of the monster. A small door in the monster's back was opened and the figures disappeared inside.

After some clambering about, Snatcher reached the monster's brain and set about studying the controls.

'They may be very primitive people but they could teach

us a thing or two. Gristle, them's the levers what make the legs work. Start walkin'!'

Gristle did as he was told, there was some clunking, and the giant figure of the monster moved to the water's edge and started to paddle out to sea. Soon it had passed out of the lagoon and was waist-deep in seawater.

Waist-deep in seawater

'Master, some of 'em down below is getting very wet. Any chance we could get a bit shallower?'

'Tell 'em to hold their breath and remember the mutiny laws. I wouldn't want to have to chuck anybody out in these shark-infested waters.'

There were no more complaints.

Kipper had finished his third plate of ribs and sweet potato and Arthur had eaten at least two pineapples when Queen Flo arose to speak.

'We are going into the Cabbage Forest tonight not long after the rains. This we don't normally do, but we've a lot of flowers to collect. I'll issue you all with umbrellas to keep off any drips. Be careful! The ground will be wet and if you lick your toes it would be very dangerous. We'll go for a paddle in the sea afterwards to be on the safe side. Now please follow me.'

She led them to a hut stacked full of homemade umbrellas and everybody took one. They all formed a line with the Queen at its head and they set off into the darkness of the forest. Arthur could only just see Kipper in front of him in the gloom and he almost fell over a number of times as the ground was uneven and roots crossed the path. After a few minutes the Queen called out and the line stopped.

'It's about to start. Put up your umbrellas please.'

As they put them up Arthur asked, 'What is about to start?'

The heavens opened

But before anybody could answer him the heavens opened and the heaviest rain Arthur had ever encountered started. The noise was deafening and when the rain hit the ground it bounced almost to waist height.

Then as suddenly as it started . . . it stopped.

The air now felt very damp and warm, and there was a smell of vegetables.

'Does it do this every night?' Arthur asked.

'As regularly as the sun rises.'

'So is it safe now to start collecting the flowers?'

'NO! We have to wait until most of the dripping stops and even then there is a chance one of us could be poisoned. A single drip reaching your mouth would be enough . . . '

Arthur and his friends closed their mouths very tightly and made sure they were right under their umbrellas. The Queen saw their unease and smiled.

'It's safe where we're standing, but once I take you past the next stream the Black Cabbage trees start and you have to be very, very careful. Keep your umbrellas up and look for the purple flowers beneath the trees. If you find some, only pick one flower from each clump. That way they'll have a chance to grow back again.'

'How'll we see them in this dark?'

'You will, don't worry. Follow me!'

She led the nervous line over a stream towards the deadly dripping trees.

Arthur felt an umbrella bang into his from behind. It was Fish. The boxtroll was looking nervous, and obviously trying to stay as close as possible to Arthur.

Arthur considered reassuring his friend but instead decided to keep his mouth tight shut as every few seconds a light patter sounded as a drip landed on his umbrella.

Then something miraculous happened. Spots of pale purple light started to glow under the trees.

'Is that the flowers glowing?' Marjorie asked from between pursed lips.

'Yes. Beautiful, isn't it. They glow as they produce the antidote,' the Queen replied.

'They glow as they produce the antidote'

No one talked as they moved through the forest collecting the flowers. Arthur did get very scared when a breeze hit the trees above and a shower of drips rained down on his umbrella, but he managed to avoid any splashes.

Queen Flo collected the gathered flowers from everyone and when she thought they had enough led them quietly out of the forest and back to the beach for a paddle.

When their feet were washed of any poison, they walked up the beach and turned in for the night. New hammocks had been slung between the palm trees for the crew and it was a beautiful place to sleep.

'If things were different,' Arthur said to Willbury, 'it would the most perfect night in the whole world.'

Willbury agreed. 'It's not something I shall ever forget. Imagine us sleeping on a tropical island beach under the stars.'

The gentle breeze from the sea rustled the palm leaves above them, and the breaking of the waves lulled them slowly to sleep. It was glorious, and still no one noticed that the monster was gone.

NOGENS SENTENTIA PRO IGNARUS

1 GROAT

·Ratbridge·Gazette·

Trap Snaps on 'Cheesy Crims'!

Last night in a sting operation the police captured all but the very last of the 'Cheesy Crims'. Under the guidance of the RWCA a trap was baited with a humanely tethered cheese to capture the last of the miscreants that have been terrorizing our local cheeses. At around 9.15 p.m. a small mob headed towards the marshes in search of their poor victims, but were surprised when they fell into a covered pit. The police then tried to arrest the mob. In the melee one particularly evil 'Cheesy Crim' managed to escape.

'We chased him into the woods but he disappeared down a Trotting Badger hole, and escaped. We would have followed him, but it was felt that there was too great a risk of badger attack, so orders were given to hold back.

'We did however get a good look at him and have published a description.'

The man is described as sprightly, about 70 years old, some 5' 7" tall, with a thick beard, and wearing a tartan dressing gown with a woolly hat.

Here at the Gazette we are offering a reward of 2000 groats for the capture of this last blaggard.

Guillemot's twenty-four hour beach supermarket

Chapter 5

THE SUPERMARKET

Guillemot closed and locked the doors of the twenty-four hour beach supermarket at seven p.m. He'd had enough. It had been a hard day at the till and even with the mirrors placed around the store and a sharp eye, Guillemot had lost at least three shopping baskets, two boxes of postcards, and various other small items. This was not how he had thought his life on a south-sea paradise was going to be.

After a quick meal made up of the latest date-expired food items he climbed the steps to the roof. Here he would sit, watch the sun go down, and use the last of the light to prepare his catapult for anybody who tried to break in.

Once the sun set he relied on burglar-alarms and traps to dissuade the intruders. These worked so well that he'd not lost any stock for three nights.

Guillemot poured himself a large coconut cocktail and

sat back to wait for the first of the burglars. As he sipped he daydreamed of getting away from this miserable island, perhaps retiring to a little country cottage in England and never having to deal with shoplifters again. Then his attention turned to how the attack would come tonight.

'They're so unimaginative. I wish they would come up with something original.'

A bush moved slowly across the sands towards the supermarket.

'Not again!' he muttered as he took a coconut from a large pile by his sun-lounger and fired it at the bush. There was a scream and the bush ran away cursing.

The bush ran away cursing

'And I hope your nest is struck by lightning!' he called back.

He took another sip and sat back to wait for the next attempt. After his alarm had gone off three times, and he had emptied the trap pits twice he managed to get an hour's sleep.

Then something woke him. He felt uneasy, but was not

sure why as the alarms were silent and there were no signs of bushes.

He looked over the edge of his stockade. No one was trying to tunnel in, and the traps were empty.

'Something's up. I just know it.'

After wandering around the store he climbed back on the roof and sat down again. Then he saw it. Coming towards the island was the monster the cabbage islanders used to scare off outsiders.

'I wonder what they want?' Then he smiled. 'Maybe they want to buy something!' He put down his catapult and decided to go down to meet his possible customers.

The monster was on the beach and had come to a stop by the time Guillemot reached it. He was now rubbing his hands at the thought of making some money.

The small door opened and started to disgorge some highly disreputable-looking characters. Most of them were soaked through and gasping for breath—clearly they had spent impressive amounts of time under water while moving the monster through the sea. The largest and most ferocious-looking of them, a large man with an eye patch, had no such difficulties—he was not at all out of breath and was completely bone dry—obviously, Guillemot thought, he must have stayed well out of trouble in the head of the monster.

As the men gathered themselves and began to recover from their underwater ordeal, Guillemot stared. They weren't islanders! In fact they looked English. Yes, he was sure of it. The pale skin, the miserable look, the dirty ill-fitting clothes. Yes! They must be his countrymen.

He rushed forward.

'Excuse me. Are you English?'

The large man with the eye patch looked him up and down. 'Yes. And are you Guillemot of Guillemot's Fairtrade botanicals and knick-knacks?'

'Are you Guillemot of Guillemot's Fairtrade botanicals and knick-knacks?'

The islanders must have told these men of another of their countrymen. 'Yes, sir. And who am I addressing?'

'One of your customers. Archibald Snatcher esquire.'

Guillemot was shocked and not sure quite what to do. It crossed his mind that Archibald Snatcher esquire had come to complain—but he had sent him his order of Black Cabbage Seeds and the seeds really did what he said in his advertisements. He decided that it was best just to play along for the moment.

'At your service.'

'At your service,' said Guillemot, giving a bow. 'Your order? It did arrive safely?'

'Oh, yes.'

'And you were happy with it?'

'Very much so. We'd like some more, a lot more. So we thought we'd come in person. Deal direct if you get my meaning. But we have a few problems. I don't think the producers are going to co-operate with supplying our requirements. That is why we're here. We thought you might be able to help us.'

Snatcher gave Guillemot a wink with his good eye. 'I think we might need a bit of extra manpower to get things done.'

Guillemot was starting to get the picture. 'Did you "borrow" the monster?'

'Yes.'

'And were its owners aware of this?'

'Not exactly.'

Guillemot smiled. He didn't like his own islanders, but he disliked the other islanders more. 'So you need help in, shall we say, "fulfilling" your order?'

'Exactly. It might take rather a robust approach.'

Guillemot could see that this could be the chance he'd wished for. That island was rich with things he could trade. And what was more, if he played his cards right he could make some money from this 'Snatcher' in the process.

'So you would like me to provide you with the means to collect what you're after? Perhaps some hired help?'

'Exactly. I think we understand each other very well.'

'And what might you be willing to pay?'

Snatcher liked this man. 'Are you interested in a job?'

'What kind of job?

'One that might be very, very lucrative.'

Guillemot could smell money.

'Once we get what we want we'll be off back to England, but we'll still need more seed. I'll need all I can get, and I need someone here in charge.'

'You're on!'

'So can you provide the help?' Snatcher demanded.

'I think so. It might take a few trinkets. The people around here won't get out of bed unless there is something in it for them.'

Snatcher had a think. 'Is there anything we might offer them?'

'It's really easy. All you have to do is make them want something they don't have. What have you got?'

This baffled Snatcher. He didn't have anything. Was there anything he'd brought with him? Then he remembered . . .

'Do you think they'd like some trotting badgers?'

Guillemot's face dropped. 'Trotting badgers? You've brought trotting badgers halfway around the world?'

'Yes.'

Guillemot thought. If he was on the other island and well out of the way, then he'd rather enjoy the idea of the trotting badgers wreaking havoc on his old 'trading partners'.

'We just have to work out the angle.'

Guillemot's face dropped

Once Only Special Offer!

Advance Orders Taken!

Very Limited Supply!

No Cash Needed!

**BUY NOW!
PAY LATER!**

Chapter 6

THE HARD SELL

Next morning a very large sign hung over the door of the beach supermarket.

Once Only Special Offer!

Advance Orders Taken!

Very Limited Supply!

No Cash Needed!

BUY NOW! PAY LATER!

At nine o'clock, unobserved by anyone, a solitary islander approached the shop, read the sign and disappeared again. Fifteen minutes later, Snatcher, who was waiting inside the

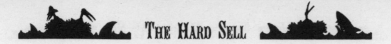

shop with Guillemot and the rest of the crew, heard a sound that at first he couldn't make out. It sounded like a cross between a repeated war cry and a relentless squawking. Then, as the sound got louder and clearer, he smirked. Guillemot's sign had done its job.

'SHOP! SHOP! SHOP! SHOP! SHOP! SHOP! SHOP! SHOP! SHOP! SHOP! SHOP! SHOP!'

Snatcher peered out of the shop door to see the approaching islanders—and got a huge surprise. They were large birds, the size of turkeys, swathed in jewellery and hats, and each carrying a large shopping basket.

Each carrying a large shopping basket

'SHOP! SHOP! SHOP! SHOP! SHOP! SHOP! SHOP! SHOP! SHOP! SHOP! SHOP! SHOP!'

The clamouring mass of shopping birds came towards the supermarket.

Gristle spoke. 'Look at 'em all. Loads of them! Do yer think they will be any good in a fight?'

'Not sure,' muttered Snatcher. 'But might be good roasted.'

'SHOP! SHOP! SHOP! SHOP! SHOP! SHOP! SHOP! SHOP! SHOP! SHOP! SHOP! SHOP!'

The birds stopped and fell silent as Guillemot raised a hand.

'As you may have heard I have a very special offer today, and for one day only. A shipment of unequalled value is arriving and it falls to me to offer advance orders. What is more I am not asking for money now . . . or ever!'

The birds started clucking in surprise. It was not what they had come to expect from Guillemot.

'No. What I am asking is for you to sign up to give me just a little help with collection. You'll receive some truly remarkable items and you will be at liberty to do what you want with them. Do I have any takers?'

There was a single squawk of 'YES!' and this set off all the other birds. Guillemot raised his hand again and shouted.

'QUIET! If you want to take advantage of this offer I insist that you form a queue!'

A disorderly queue formed at the gate. There was a lot of pecking as birds tried to outmanoeuvre each other to get closer to the front of the queue.

It only took half an hour to sign them all up, each bird making a beak print on a piece of paper. Snatcher and Gristle were put in charge of this as Guillemot was trying to stop the birds from stealing things from his shelves. This was

difficult as the shop was packed and the birds were taking full advantage. After a while Guillemot just stood at the door and patted down the leaving birds and made them raise their wings. He still lost a lot of stock.

It only took half an hour to sign them all up

By eleven, nine hundred birds had signed up and were waiting outside on the beach.

'I think you'd better tell them what they've got to do,' said Guillemot.

'Yes,' smiled Snatcher. 'By the way, Guillemot. Can they fly?'

'No.'

'So how do they get from island to island?'

'Boats. Well, I say boats. More like rafts . . . well actually more like big nests. They use their wings as paddles.'

'Is that how you got across to the other island?'

'Yes. It's not very dignified, but it works. Lost a couple of nests to sharks but I was in the biggest nest and there were no problems.'

There were no problems

'Didn't that upset the birds?'

'Not really. Any chance they get to inherit each other's things is seen as positive.'

Snatcher walked outside. He had the measure of the birds.

'Right then. We're off on a little shopping trip.' This was greeted by approving clucking.

'On the other island over there are your new purchases. I'll need a little help getting you your orders.'

'What we got to do?' called out one of the birds.

'It is like this,' explained Snatcher. 'The people on that island might stand in the way when they see what a bargain you're getting. They might put up a fight to stop you getting what's coming to you.'

The birds started squawking in outrage. They liked a

fight but usually only got the chance at the opening of the January sales.

'As you may have noticed we have borrowed their walking monster. We're now going to walk back and I'll need you lot to follow so you can get your bargains. Do you think you can manage that?'

'After the fight do we get our special offer?'

'Oh yes!' smiled Snatcher.

NOGENS SENTENTIA PRO IGNARUS

1 GROAT

THE ·Ratbridge·Gazette·

LONE CHEESE FIEND EVADES CAPTURE

The net is closing as the 'house to house' search continues by day, but by night the fiend is still driven by his evil desires. Police and dogs chased the fiend back into the woods last night after he emerged on what was thought to be yet another of his evil forays. He again escaped down one of the badger tunnels, but not before losing his woolly hat.

In a statement from police it was postulated that this last miscreant had avoided detection by making sure he was free of cheese traces before returning to his lair, thus avoiding detection. But with the woolly hat the police now think they have all they need to trace and forensically link the criminal to the crimes. Large numbers of police are being drafted in from across the county to assist in the sweep of the town and it is thought that by tomorrow night the fiend will be in custody.

The courts of justice have issued a statement that this last and most evil of the 'Cheesy Crims' will receive the heaviest of sentences and that no mercy will be shown.

We here at the Gazette say 'HEAR! HEAR!'

Suddenly he felt himself pick up speed and rush towards the beach

Chapter 7

THE QUIET BEFORE THE STORM

Arthur was woken by the sun shining on his face. He jumped out of his hammock, feeling totally refreshed after a night in the open air. Smiling, he gazed out towards their ship. It floated calmly in the lagoon and looked at peace.

'I think I will start my day with a swim.' He lifted his clothes over his head, rushed over the sand, and dived in.

Coming up for air, he thought he might try to catch a wave, and body surf in. He had seen some of the island children doing it yesterday and it looked fun. So he swam out a little further. When he saw a wave coming he turned and prepared to catch it. The wave reached him and he paddled as fast as he could. Suddenly he felt himself pick

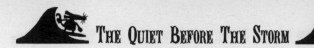

up speed and rush towards the beach. As he did he noticed something was missing.

At first he was not sure what it was, then it struck him. The monster had gone. He wondered if the islanders had moved it. Then he saw Fish come down to the beach. He called out to him.

'Come in and try riding a wave.'

Fish didn't need to be asked twice. As they played, more and more of their friends came to join them in the water. Tom discovered that he could get a very good ride standing on Kipper's stomach and soon all the rats were riding on bellies.

Tom discovered that he could get a very good ride standing on Kipper's stomach

The noise didn't take long to wake the islanders. But when the first of them came down they also noticed the lack of monster. Instead of joining the surfers, they ran back to the village to sound the alarm. Arthur and the other surfers saw that something was up and gathered on the beach. Soon the islanders arrived.

'This is bad. It takes quite a few people to operate the monster,' observed Queen Flo.

'And I have a funny feeling I know who they are,' added Bert. 'Shall I go and check?'

'Yes. I think you better had.'

Bert climbed the rock and looked down the hole

They all watched as Bert ran across the beach and over to the rocks where the cave was. Bert climbed the rock and looked down the hole. There was the ladder. He signalled a 'thumbs down'.

'I think we have our answer,' said Willbury.

'What do you think that Snatcher is going to do?' asked the Queen.

'Whatever it is, it'll not be good. That you can count on.'

'Where do you think he's gone?'

'The other island. There is nowhere else he could have gone without the ship,' offered Arthur.

'Yup!' said Kipper. 'And he'll be back for the ship and I reckon he might come after the Black Cabbage Seeds as well.'

Bert stood and drew out his sword. 'Well we won't give them to him.'

'Knowing Snatcher he will use any means he can to get what he wants. Are there any weapons on the other island?' asked Arthur.

'No. Just an awful lot of awful birds.'

'What about the shoppers you were telling us about?'

'They are the shoppers.'

'Yes. And how!' answered the Queen as she shook her head.

'Would they help Snatcher?'

'Only if they thought something was in it for them.'

'Well I think we should expect the worst,' said Willbury sadly.

'We can fight Snatcher and his mob . . . and a bunch of birds.' Kipper tried to lift spirits.

'You have to remember that they have our monster, and might have an awful lot of awful big birds, with awful big sharp beaks.'

'What's more we don't know how to fight. We only scare people away,' said the Queen.

'Come on, everyone, we can do it!' said Bert. 'We've been in a fight or two. It's only Snatcher . . . and a bunch of birds . . . and a monster . . . And Snatcher's men, of course . . . How many birds?'

'Could be as many as a thousand.'

Even Bert was silent. Everyone looked at each other in dismay.

Then Marjorie spoke. 'Well, they are going to come if we are ready or not. So it might be better to be as prepared as we can. Any ideas?'

'How many birds?'

Bert was stationed with a telescope in the crow's nest of the ship

Chapter 8

THE BATTLE OF THE BEACH

Everybody mucked in. There was an awful lot to be done if they were to stand any chance of repelling an attack.

To get as early a warning as possible Bert was stationed with a telescope in the crow's nest of the ship. It was agreed that he would signal to the beach as soon as he saw anything.

Arthur was to watch for the signal from Bert, and he was hidden with Fish up a tree on the edge of the beach.

'I hope Snatcher doesn't come back,' he said nervously.

Fish looked gloomy. The prospect of a battle had brought his mood down.

All about below, there were frenetic preparations for what was to come. The pirates and rats searched every corner of the ship for weapons of any sort. Swords, knives, and even wooden spoons were collected and rowed back to the beach. There were not enough to go round so they made spears from bamboo that grew near the beach, clubs from suitable pieces of driftwood, and battleaxes from sticks and anything sharp they could find.

Bert saw that Marjorie was standing on the beach thinking. 'What's up?'

'I think we could handle Snatcher and his mob in a fair fight, but with them having the monster they have the advantage. We have to slow it down or stop it.'

'What should we do?'

'Build defences.'

'Let's get to it then!'

Marjorie told Bert to gather everyone they could including the children and soon homemade shovels and coconut shell 'diggers' were hard at work with sand flying everywhere.

Soon homemade shovels and coconut shell 'diggers' were hard at work

After an hour Marjorie said that it might also be very dangerous for the children to be on the beach when the attack came so they were gathered up and led away to safety deep in the jungle.

Once the children had gone a gloom set over the beach and work slowed, until Willbury arrived with some of the villagers who had prepared 'Battle Rations'. This was a very large tray of coconut shells filled with the last of the chocolate from the ship mixed with hot coconut milk and honey. It tasted very good and filled them with new energy as they dug. Soon Marjorie declared the front defences were ready.

'I think they will do. Now it is time to build personal defences and wait.'

'Personal defences?' asked Kipper.

'Yes. You should be good at this. Everybody make themselves a sandcastle big enough to hide behind.'

As the sun grew hotter the beach became dotted with mounds of sand.

The beach became dotted with mounds of sand

Kipper, who had proved Marjorie correct about his talents at sandcastle building, had even built an extension to his castle using palm fronds so he could keep in the shade while waiting. This was copied by the others, and as it reached midday it became very quiet on the beach as everyone settled to wait in the shade behind their personal defences.

In the crow's nest Bert was sweltering and very uncomfortable under an umbrella. He was trying to keep his tail in the shade. He'd been hanging it over the side of the barrel in the wind but with the strong sun it had burnt and the skin under the thin hairs was already starting to peel. His mother had warned him about burning his tail but the cool breeze had seemed so tempting. After tipping a little water from a drinking flask over it he resumed his watch and slowly swung his telescope across the horizon.

Tipping a little water from a drinking flask

There it was! It was still a few miles away but the monster was coming. He took a small mirror from his pocket and checked the position of the sun. Then he signalled to Arthur. The sun's beams reflected off the mirror and Bert could see a spot of brighter light on the palm tree below where he knew Arthur was. He moved the mirror and the flash of light flickered over Arthur.

Arthur was startled as the flash of light almost blinded him. Then he realized it was the signal. 'He's seen them. He's seen them. They're coming!'

'Signal back to Bert to let him know you've seen his signal,' called Kipper.

Arthur flashed his mirror back at Bert.

Bert saw the reply and then turned back to watch the approaching attack. He could clearly see the monster and behind it an armada of small boats. As they got closer Bert saw what type of boats they were and what was in the boats.

'My sainted aunt! It's the birds. Blooming loads of them! And in blooming floating nests.'

'Blooming loads of them!'

Paddling with wings and simple oars the birds were doing their best to keep up with the mighty monster, but not all of them were faring so well. The swell was having a bad effect on the nest boats and the smaller and more badly built were coming apart and dumping their crew in the sea. Bert noticed that this didn't seem to worry those in the better boats who paddled on without them.

The swell was having a bad effect on the nest boats

Bert looked from the weird armada to the beach. Against the monster and the huge number of birds, his friends' preparations looked puny.

'I think they might need my help. Time for a swim!' and with that he launched himself from the crow's nest, plunged down into the sea, and started swimming as fast as he could for the beach.

Arthur watched Bert as he flew from the crow's nest and then swam towards them, then he turned his attention as the others did to the rapidly approaching monster and nest boats. The monster reached the gap in the reef and more of the nests broke up in the surf there, but there were still hundreds of them and even the shipwrecked birds were trailing along behind.

'Stay out of sight and keep quiet!' Marjorie called.

Closer and closer they came. As they reached the shallows the monster rose higher in the water and its legs became visible as it paddled its way towards them. Bert was now only yards ahead in the water and as he reached the sand Kipper broke the silence and called out to him.

'Bert! Over here quick!'

'Bert! Over here quick!'

The wet rat ran up the beach and dived behind Kipper's sandcastle.

'I don't know if we are ever going to be able to stop that thing. But I am ready for a fight,' Bert panted.

Then the monster stopped. Arthur saw the glint of metal somewhere on the top of the monster's head. A blade, pushed through from inside, and cutting a flap in the fabric skin. Snatcher's head appeared through the hole, followed by an arm with a megaphone.

Snatcher's head appeared followed by an arm with a megaphone

'Morning! I know you're there, I can sees you from up here. Me and my friends—' at this point he pointed at the mass of floating birds and nest boats that bobbed around him—''ve come to get a few things and if you keep out of our way, there will be no trouble. We might even spare a few lives. But if you don't play along, we is going to give you all a very hard time.'

Kipper and Tom came out from behind their sandcastles. Both had large spears and swords.

'If you don't disappear you will discover you have bitten off more than you can chew,' said Tom bravely.

'That's not the way to speak to a man in control of a sixty-foot monster and a bunch of vicious bird warriors.'

'What!' Kipper scoffed. 'That bunch of turkeys?'

Kipper hadn't quite realized the effect this insult would have on the wet birds. They were furious. No sooner were the words out than the birds started puffing up their chests, flapping their wings and squawking very rude squawks. Even the sound of surf was drowned out by the noise. Kipper and Tom ran back behind their defences.

The combination of the rough journey, Kipper's insult, and the thought that someone was standing in the way of a bargain that was rightfully theirs, was all too much for the birds. They could hold back no longer.

'ATTACK! ATTACK! ATTACK! ATTACK!'

Snatcher had not intended it to go quite this way but there was little he could do about it so he watched as the birds stormed the beach.

The birds leaped ashore and made for the sandcastles where Tom and Kipper were hiding. But as they crossed the high water mark something they were not expecting happened. The birds disappeared.

Marjorie had designed a trap. This consisted of a disguised trench about five feet deep, covered with palm fronds and sand. As soon as the first of the birds realized that they were dropping into a pit they panicked, but this had no effect as the birds behind were so angry that they just charged on. Soon all the birds had disappeared, and the second part of the plan came into action.

The trench trap

'Nets!' shouted Marjorie.

From the cover of the trees, islanders and pirates ran forward pulling nets to seal the birds in. Once the nets were over the trench, rats appeared from holes in the sand and pegged them down.

There was a cheer from Arthur and his friends.

Snatcher watched in disgust.

'Right you lot. You leave me with no choice. I am just going to have to flatten you all.' He looked back down inside the head and bellowed. 'Start the legs and prepare for lunch!'

The monster moved onto the sand and easily stepped right over the trench. Up the tree Arthur could feel the stomp of each footfall.

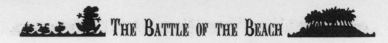

The monster moved onto the sand

'Pull!' shouted Marjorie as she set in motion the next part of their plan.

Several yards back in the forest ropes were cut and coconut trees that had been bent over with winches were released. As the trees sprang up they released coconuts, which flew through the air and hit their target. The monster screamed in several places and looked rather punctured . . .

. . . but still it came on.

The monster screamed in several places and looked rather punctured

Marjorie shouted again. 'Operation Lace-up, GO!'

A very long length of rope had been looped around the beach and hidden under the sand. The ends of the rope were being held by two groups of the burliest pirates who, on the command to go, started to pull in the rope. The rope lifted from the sand and caught around the monster's legs.

The monster wavered slightly as the rope pulled tightly round its legs—but then somehow managed to keep moving shakily forwards.

The rope lifted from the sand and caught around the monster's legs

'Keep pulling!'

Seeing that the monster seemed unaffected, the islanders ran to join the pirates at each end of the rope. The rope pulled tighter still and for a moment the monster stopped.

Inside, Snatcher was screaming at his crew. 'If yer don't make this thing walk again I will have your guts for garters!'

This seemed to do the trick. The legs strained at the rope and with a loud pop, the rope snapped and the two teams pulling on the ends fell to the ground.

The two teams pulling on the ends fell to the ground

'What now?' Kipper shouted to Marjorie.

Marjorie looked distraught. 'I . . . I . . . don't know.'

'We have to do something.'

'Yes, but what?'

Arthur felt Fish pull at his sleeve. The boxtroll wanted to tell him something but didn't have the words. Fish pointed to himself then Arthur, and then to the ground.

'You want me to come with you?'

Fish nodded and quickly shinned down the tree. When they reached the ground Fish looked across at the monster and then to one piece of the broken rope. Then he did something Arthur didn't expect.

Fish ran from the cover of the trees, grabbed the rope and tied a large loop in it. When he'd done this he looked up at the monster. The monster's left foot was about to land only a few feet from the boxtroll.

With enormous courage Fish suddenly threw himself to the ground and rolled right under the foot as it fell. The foot landed . . . but Fish had escaped and was now standing on the other side of it. The loop was now around the monster's foot and Fish pulled it tight.

Arthur watched as Fish ran along the beach to the free end of the rope. He picked it up and dived into the waves.

He picked it up and dived into the waves

As he did he waved to Arthur to join him. Arthur rushed past the monster and ran into the surf. Fish held the rope high and pointed to the ship.

'I get it! You want us to take the rope out to the ship?'

Fish nodded. Arthur grabbed onto the rope and they began to swim.

Kipper and Tom saw what was happening.

'We need to cause a distraction,' shouted Kipper.

'Got any ideas?'

But before they could come up with anything the monster started to bend over and open its mouth. Kipper looked up and saw something horrid.

'Look! It's got new teeth. Sharp metal ones . . . And they are coming this way.'

The jaws of the monster started to close. Kipper saw it happening and quick as a flash took his thick bamboo spear and forced it between the roof of the monster's mouth and just behind its lower dentures.

Quick as a flash

The jaws locked. Tom and Kipper were inside the monster's mouth and could hear Snatcher shouting.

'Raise up the head and chomp them up a bit!'

They rose, but the chomping wasn't working.

'What's going on? Why aren't you chomping them?'

'The jaws are stuck!'

'Apply more pressure!'

Kipper and Tom saw the spear begin to bend.

'It's going to give!'

Tom was holding his spear and pushed it into position alongside the first.

The jaws stopped moving again and there was cursing from somewhere inside the head.

'SONS OF CHEESE THIEVING VERMIN!!!!'

Kipper smiled to Tom. 'He is mad isn't he?'

The spears started to bend.

'More pressure!' screamed Snatcher.

Out in the waves Arthur and Fish heard the twang as the drive belt that drove the jaws broke and the monster's mouth fell open. Kipper and Tom started to fall but as they did Kipper grabbed onto the large cloth tongue with one hand and Tom with the other.

Their friends on the beach held their breath.

'Crawl up my arm!' shouted Kipper as they dangled from the monster's mouth. Tom climbed for all he was worth.

Inside the monster's brain, Snatcher screamed. 'Gristle! Fix those blooming jaws!'

Gristle unbuckled his belt and, as his trousers dropped, managed to tighten it around the cogs that drove the jaws.

Arthur watched, horrified, as the monster's teeth snapped together and a large bump slid down its throat and swelled its belly. But then a sword poked through the wall of the tummy and split to reveal Tom and Kipper, who then jumped to the sand and ran to join their friends, who were so relieved that they let out a cheer.

A large bump slid down the monster's throat

'That was close!'

'You are telling me. I thought we had seen the last of you.'

'You should be so lucky.'

Arthur and Fish clambered aboard the ship still clutching the rope.

'What are we going to do?'

Fish waved to Arthur to follow him. The boxtroll fed the rope around one of the winches and fixed it.

'You are going to wind him in?'

They both grabbed the spars of the winch and started to push

Fish smiled. They both grabbed the spars of the winch and started to push. Quickly the slack in the rope wound in. Then almost as soon as the rope was tight a gentle breeze came up from the west and started to push against the ship. This tightened the rope even more and began to pull on the monster's leg.

'What's happening? I didn't tell you to turn this thing around,' snapped Snatcher to Gristle.

'I ain't doing nothing!'

'Well how come we is turning round?'

'I'm not sure. Why don't you have a look upstairs?' Gristle pointed at the hole in the top of the monster's head.

Snatcher looked out.

'OH MY GAWD! They got us tied to the ship and is pulling us out.'

'What do you want us to do?'

Snatcher could see that if he resisted the ship and the rope didn't snap they would be pulled over.

'Turn out to sea and start walking!'

There was renewed cheering as the monster retreated back into the sea.

'Well done, Arthur and Fish!'

Snatcher was reassessing the situation.

'OK then. I get to control the ship and by the look of it I might get a couple of hostages out of it this way. Not so bad. I might enjoy a little punishing of hostages!'

He looked down inside the head.

'Right, lads! I think I've just sorted things. Make ready for boarding.'

The monster retreated back into the sea

NOGENS SENTENTIA PRO IGNARUS

1 GROAT

THE ·Ratbridge·Gazette·

LATE EXTRA

Mass Breakout Of Cheese Crims Causes Panic!

While police were conducting their sweep of the whole town in the search for the last cheese fiend, the other 'Cheese Crims' housed at Ratbridge gaol rioted, smashed down the gates, escaped and are even now causing panic across the town. The mob seems to be moving towards the cheese marshes in an attempt to satisfy their lust.

Lock yourselves in your homes until the mob is quelled!

The monster loomed towards the ship

Chapter 9

UNDER NEW MANAGEMENT

The monster loomed towards the ship and as it did Arthur and Fish went from feelings of triumph to fear of what would happen when the monster arrived.

'What are we going to do?' exclaimed Arthur.

Fish looked worried and clueless.

'I don't think we will be able to defend the ship so I think we better swim for it! Over the side!'

They both climbed on the rail, jumped, and swam wide of the monster and headed for the beach. As they swam, Arthur looked back and saw Snatcher and his men climbing from the head of the monster and jumping down onto the ship.

They both swam wide of the monster and headed for the beach

'I am not sure that was such a good idea,' he called over to Fish, suddenly realizing that they might have made things even worse.

Despite this they were met with cheers as they reached the beach.

'Well done Fish, and Arthur!' called out Willbury. 'You've saved us!'

'I am not sure that we have really helped. Snatcher has taken control of the ship,' replied Arthur.

'Snatcher has taken control of the ship!'

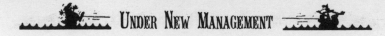

A solemn silence fell over the beach. As they gazed out across the water they could just make out the forms of Snatcher and his mob standing on deck and they seemed to be laughing.

'Now what?' asked Kipper.

On board, Snatcher started dishing out orders.

'Strip down the monster and stow it. I think it will be very useful when we get back to Blighty. And Gristle . . . get me some paper and a quill.'

Gristle lowered himself over the stern to the captain's cabin, then returned back up the rope.

'The smell down there is awful. I think one of the trotting badgers must have food poisoning.'

'Ah yes, the dear trotting badgers. I'll have to include them in the deal.'

'What deal?'

'Well, we have the ship and if our friends want to get home they will have to do exactly what I tell them. This is going to be fun.'

'If our friends want to get home they will have to do exactly what I tell them'

For the next hour or so, Snatcher sat writing and rewriting a letter of terms. When it was done he was looking very pleased with himself and chuckled as he poked the letter into a bottle and pushed in a cork.

'Gristle. Swim ashore and parley with them blighters.'

'What, me?'

'Yes, you!'

Gristle could see that there was no way of getting out of it.

'What do you want me to say?'

'Nothing. Just give 'em the bottle and wait for the reply. It is going to be a joy to behold.'

'This is outrageous!'

Chapter 10

DEAL OR NO DEAL

'This is outrageous!' Willbury snorted after briefly inspecting the letter Gristle had just handed him.

Gristle didn't know quite how to react. His boss had the upper hand, but here he was at the mercy of the enemy. He decided it was best to look at what remained of his old boots.

'What does Snatcher say?' asked Tom.

'Quite a lot. And most of it unrepeatable.'

'Is it some kind of deal?'

'For him it is. I'll read it out . . . apart from the rude bits at the beginning, and end . . . and a few bits in the middle.'

'Let's hear it then,' sighed Marjorie.

'Dear bunch of misfits, failed lawyers, pathetic pirates, filthy rats, and other assorted losers, if you ever wish to see England again you'll follow the following instructions to the letter. Please deliver to the ship the following:

'One: Enough food and water for the journey home. It won't be necessary to provide much for any of you lot who want to come with us, as prisoners will be on quarter rations. Provisions will include at least ten cheeses from the forest and as much fuel as can be gathered and stowed.

'Two: One ton of Black Cabbage seed.'

'What does he want that lot for? It takes less than one seed to poison someone.' Queen Flo was outraged.

Willbury shook his head. 'I think there's no helping the man.'

'Or most of England if he gets hold of that stuff,' added Arthur.

Willbury continued reading.

'Three: Signed statements from everybody wishing to return to England, admitting mutiny.'

'If we agreed to that we could all end up in prison or transported,' scoffed Bert.

'in prison or transported'

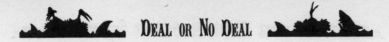

'I know, but if we're to get back we might just have to take our chance. I doubt very much if Snatcher is going to want to have a lot to do with the legal system back home, but it would be a huge risk.' Willbury did not look happy, but went on.

'In addition to the above, agreement to the following:

'Four: That everybody who wishes to travel home will submit to a search, to make sure they are not carrying any Un-Cabbage Flowers or weapons.

'Five: That all prisoners will sign another undertaking not to mention any details of this trip to anyone, and failure to do so will lead to loss of all personal possessions.

'Six: This contract will stand under the statutes of English, International, and Island law.'

'So if we sign we get to go home, but heaven knows what will happen when we get there?' said Marjorie.

'You never know what Snatcher might have got planned for us on the way home, either. Once we are on the ship we would be at his mercy,' added Bert.

'Why don't we just wait until the next ship comes along?' asked Kipper.

'We could do, but if we stay here we have no idea when we might get home, and what we'll find when we get there,' said Willbury. 'With all those cabbage seeds Snatcher could cause untold mayhem.'

'And if he takes that monster back too, he'll be unstoppable,' Bert added.

'And I need to get back to Grandfather!' said Arthur urgently. 'I can't leave him alone, especially if Snatcher is going back to cause more trouble.'

'Anyway,' said Marjorie firmly, 'we can't do what he asks. There's just no way we can hand over wild cheeses, or the cabbage seeds.'

'If you want to go home you's going to have to accept the lot,' Gristle muttered.

Queen Flo spoke again. 'We haven't actually seen any wild cheeses for at least two years. Tell Snatcher if he wants the cheeses he might have to wait a long, long time.'

Gristle looked worried. 'He ain't goin' to like that.'

'Would you mind leaving us alone for a few minutes?'

Gristle wandered off to poke the trapped shopping birds with a stick while the terms were discussed.

Gristle wandered off to poke the trapped shopping birds with a stick

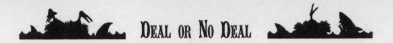

'So what do we do?'

Arthur felt awful. 'I have to go back. How can I stay here not knowing what's happening to Grandfather? Perhaps Snatcher will agree to take just me without the cheeses and the cabbage seeds.'

'If one of us goes back, we all have to,' Willbury said solemnly.

'Willbury is right,' said Bert. 'I think we will have to accept Snatcher's conditions and take our chance. There is no way Arthur can stay here while his grandfather is ill, and we all have to do our best to stop Snatcher getting loose with that monster back home.'

It seemed very sad but they'd have to aid Snatcher—at least for now.

'Then we will just have to come up with a plan to make sure we can get the better of Snatcher and his men,' said Marjorie.

'Like what?'

'I'm not sure yet, but it had better be good.'

'Like what?'

The birds were extremely unhappy

Chapter 11

PROVISIONS

The next two days were frenetic. The first job was releasing the shopping birds. The birds were extremely unhappy. Surprisingly not so much at being trapped, but at not getting the bargain deal they'd signed up for. Bert took charge of proceedings and ordered his helpers to arm themselves with their spears—but to wrap towels around one end so as not to puncture the birds. Then, while one group held down the birds with their padded spears, others released the pegs. As soon as the net was off the birds struggled so much that it became impossible to restrain them, and Bert's crew pulled back to avoid being pecked. The birds jumped out of the pit. Then they started complaining about not getting their special deal. Bert was not sure what to do and as the threat of pecking seem to have passed he guessed it would be all right just to let them wander about until hopefully they would find their way home. This didn't happen. Instead the birds got in the way of everything, and filled the air with complaints. Kipper was very tempted to insult them again when two birds started following him and telling him that if they didn't get their deal they would go to see the local trading standards officer and possibly write to the paper. Fortunately Tom stopped him in time.

'Apart from frying them, what are we going to do with them?' whispered Kipper.

'I'm not sure. They just won't stop going on about this blooming deal that Snatcher promised them,' Tom replied. 'But we've got to do something—I don't think I can stand much more of this squawking.'

'It's obvious that Snatcher offered them some sort of deal to get them to help him. He probably never intended to carry it through. Perhaps we should ask him about it. Something has to be done otherwise we are never going to get the provisions he wants onboard.'

'You are right. If he want the provisions he has to get the birds off our backs.'

Kipper and Tom took one of the fishing boats and rowed out to the ship and asked to speak to Snatcher. They waited for a minute or two then Snatcher came to the rail and eyed them up.

'What do you two want?'

'The shopping birds are causing problems with us getting your provisions ready. Since we released them, all they have done is wander about complaining about some deal you made with them and getting in the way. It's making it almost impossible to work. We wonder if you might be able to sort the situation out.'

'What do you two want?'

Snatcher smiled slyly.

'Don't worry. I can sort this. Can't have them disturbing the provisions. Just row back and tell them that they will be given everything they were promised as a big thank you for helping me out. Then use the boats to ferry them out here and we'll use the ship to take them back to their island and give them what they have got coming.'

When Kipper and Tom returned to the beach the birds were delighted with the news and without any instruction formed an excited queue at the water's edge. The complaints were now replaced with feverish speculation as to what they were about to receive, and delight at not having to travel back to their island in the nest boats.

'What do you think Snatcher is going to give them?' Arthur asked Tom.

'Whatever it is I am sure it's no real bargain.'

Quiet returned to the beach as the birds departed, and once they were aboard, the ship set off to their island. A few hours later the ship returned with only Snatcher and his crew.

On the beach the provisions stacked up and the fishing boats started to ferry them across to the ship. Arthur was aboard one of the first loads and noticed a couple of rather strange changes. The crew looked a little battered and had lots of fresh cuts and bruises, and the doors down to the Captain's cabin were open again. Gristle and some of the others were washing down the stairwell.

Gristle noticed him looking at them. 'We got rid of them badgers as well.'

This seemed a bit odd but even Arthur sighed with relief at the idea of not having to share the journey home with them.

(Little did Arthur know but only six weeks later the shopping birds would become extinct, and a few months after that, a whaling ship found a man floating in an open boat in the middle of the Pacific. The man was covered in scars and asked his rescuers if they would like to buy a vest.)

The list of provisions was ticked off as it was loaded from the beach and finally all that was left was the black cabbage seeds. There were very mixed feelings about handing these over but little else could be done if Arthur and his friends were ever to get home. The villagers had gathered sacks of seeds from the forest and there was a very ominous feeling when it became time to load them onto the boats.

Willbury watched as the heavy sacks were placed in the boats, then turned and shook his head.

With everything needed for the voyage on board, Snatcher announced they were to leave the following morning. On shore for the last night the islanders gave the prisoners a last feast. Things seemed not to have turned out well but the islanders gave their new friends as much of a party as the mood allowed. A pit was dug and large rocks taken from a fire were placed in it and then parcels of food wrapped in banana leaves were placed on the rock before the pit was filled with sand and allowed to bake for a few hours. When the food was served Arthur and his friends declared that it really was some of the best food they had ever eaten. They drank coconut shell after coconut shell of fruit juices and took it in turns to sing songs. The rats and pirates sang sea shanties and the islanders sang their own local lullabies. The singing went on long into the night, but slowly they settled in their hammocks amongst the trees for the last time.

Arthur lay looking up at the stars. It felt very strange.

Here he was in such a beautiful place, but tomorrow he and his friends were going to give themselves up to Snatcher. It was the early hours before he finally went to sleep.

At daybreak he awoke and found his friends around him, taking down their hammocks and packing up their things in silence. They finished a breakfast of fresh fruit as they knew it would be a long time till they ate so well again and then loaded up fishing boats while the islanders chatted to them and looked on. As they climbed aboard there were many hugs and quite a few tears.

Then Queen Flo spoke. 'We wish we could have met you in different circumstances, but we wish you well and hope that an opportunity to turn things around comes up.'

'We really must thank you,' replied Willbury. 'I think you know we'll be looking for every chance that comes along.'

They were searched right down to their underpants

With that the boats set off from the shore towards the ship. When they reached the ship one 'prisoner' was allowed on deck at a time, and as they were they were searched right down to their underpants to make sure that no Un-Cabbage Flowers were being hidden. The gloom on the faces of the prisoners seemed to delight Snatcher's men and they took great pleasure in poking fun at them and telling them how they would punish them if the prisoners stepped out of line. Even Bert held his tongue when Gristle made jokes about his red tail.

The fishing boats went back to the beach and the islanders returned to wave a last farewell as the anchor was raised. Arthur and his friends were sad to be leaving their island and—between the many jobs they were given—waved until the ship was long past the reef and the island was almost lost from sight.

'I am sorry we brought trouble to them,' said Arthur.

'Yes. They didn't deserve it. Perhaps they can get back to the quiet life now,' replied Willbury as he watched the disappearing island.

'I doubt it will be as quiet a life now that their monster has been taken away. Anybody might turn up.'

So the return journey began and Snatcher was revelling in his power. He was very, very careful to keep the guard on the prisoners and would have happily locked them below but he knew that his 'officers' were incapable of sailing the ship home.

'It won't stop me dropping them in the drink when we get close to home though,' he confided to Gristle. 'And the Good Doctor and Fingle might be going for a dip as well . . .'

'It won't stop me dropping them in the drink'

The ship sailed south and things got a lot rougher, both the sea, and the prisoners' treatment at the hands of the 'officers'. In the bilges it was foul, wet, and the hammocks swung so violently that it was almost impossible to sleep, so Arthur and most of his friends spent as much time on deck as possible. Only Fish seemed to revel in the high seas. He had become a true sailor.

As Arthur helped Kipper at the helm they watched Fish standing at the rail on the forecastle being washed with the spray from the waves.

'He's changed so much. It is hard to imagine any other boxtroll taking to the seas like he has,' Kipper said admiringly.

'He looks in his element. Almost as much as any of you pirates.'

'Yes. The first boxtroll pirate, and a fine one.'

'I'm not sure I'm cut out to be a pirate.'

'You're not doing too badly. There is many a man that would be proud to be able to take seas like this as well as you.' And Kipper winked at him and pointed to a couple of Snatcher's men who were looking very green.

Then in a very loud voice Kipper asked Arthur, 'Do you fancy something to eat. I could murder a bacon sandwich with lots of grease and butter.'

'Yes,' smiled Arthur. 'Followed up with a plateful of sausages and more bread dipped in dripping.'

Their guards seemed to have been affected badly by the talk of food and were now 'being ill' over the rail.

'I don't like the look of the sea you know. I think it is only just starting to get rough. Fancy a plate of fried eggs and ham?'

'Not half! And washed down with a pint of raw eggs.'

Arthur and Kipper smiled but stopped torturing their guards at this point because they were being so ill that it was a distinct possibility that one of them might fall over the side.

As they reached the Cape the sea did indeed become rougher and all but the hardest of sailors and Fish went off their food. Arthur was feeling so sick he just hung in the dark in his swaying hammock in the bilges, moaned and thought about home.

'How I wish I was back in Ratbridge,' he muttered.

'Me too!' came a weak reply from Willbury who was also too ill to go on deck.

'Do you think we will ever get there?'

'I am not sure I won't die first,' came another voice. It was a weakly moaning Marjorie.

'We are not going to die. Just think of the job we have to do and how we have to save your grandfather and the others,' came Willbury's voice from the dark again.

Arthur had indeed been trying to think of his grandfather and how he was getting on, but it was hard to concentrate with feeling so ill.

'I think I'd take the jollop if it made me feel better than this.'

There was also a terrible smell from rotting seaweed

Chapter 12

THE DOLDRUMS

For five days the weather was terrible but on the day of the sixth the sea became calmer and the sickness subsided. The ship had turned north into the Atlantic, and now with every day they sailed it became warmer again. The ship started making good time, but then they reached the doldrums.

Just east of Brazil the wind completely died away. The water became glassy, the air very hot, and very still. With the monster and all the seeds they'd packed there had not been as much space for fuel and little was left.

'What do we do, captain?' asked Kipper.

Snatcher didn't like this heat. It felt damp. There was also a terrible smell from rotting seaweed that floated all around them.

'Burn everything that we don't need.'

'What don't we need?'

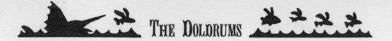

Snatcher had to think. There was almost nothing they didn't need on board if he wanted to have a monster and still be able to go through with his plan for free black jollop for all of England.

'Burn the furniture!' he ordered.

This took about a day before it was gone.

'What next?' asked Kipper.

'Burn the ship's biscuits.'

This only kept them going for three hours.

'And now, there's nothing left but your monster and the seeds?'

Snatcher's skin was coming up in heat bumps and he was sweaty and itching very badly.

'If I burn the seeds I ain't going to be able to make more poison, but if I burn the monster I won't be able to induce terror . . . This is a tricky one.' He stuck a hopeful finger in the air to see if he could feel any breeze, but all be could feel was the sun beating down on his exposed spotty red forearm.

'If we burnt a bit of the monster we might just keep going until the wind picks up,' suggested Gristle.

The over-hot and bothered Snatcher clomped Gristle around the head with the umbrella he was using as a sunshade.

'Don't be stupid. Who is going to be afraid of an almost complete monster?'

'Well, what we going to do? We could just fade away if we stay here.'

Snatcher looked from his heat bumps to the sacks of seeds.

'Maybe if we burnt just some of the seeds until the wind picked up . . . ' Making up his mind suddenly, he turned to Kipper. 'Burn five sacks of the seeds. But mind, only five sacks, and we will see where that gets us.'

Kipper smiled. A few minutes later the first of the sacks was opened and spadefuls of the seeds were shovelled into the boiler.

The fire started to roar and a thick black disgustingly smelly smoke poured out of the chimney, and the ship started to make headway again. By the time the fourth sack was burnt a change had come over everyone. Even Snatcher's heat bumps had miraculously disappeared and he was feeling very perky.

'Right! Back to Ratbridge . . . and quickly. I am feeling very peckish,' ordered Snatcher.

Marjorie sneaked up to Willbury and whispered to him. 'Do you realize what has happened?'

'Do you realize what has happened?'

'No. But I do feel oddly rather good. And there is something else. I keep thinking of my childhood . . . sitting in front of the fire eating something.' Then a look of guilty horror crossed his face. 'Slices of . . . no . . . no . . . cheese on toast!'

'It's the fumes from the seeds. It's got into us all and though it might be making us feel better it will also be poisoning us with the cheese lust.'

'What do we do?'

'I think there is only one thing we can do.'

Marjorie fetched Fish from the bow and took him down to the bilges. Then she sent for Arthur.

'I want you to bring down each of our crew and friends. Only let a few down at a time and make sure that it's not noticed.'

'Aye, aye!'

'And before you go have this.'

In the darkness of the bilges Arthur saw a large blue glowing bottle appear from under Fish's box.

A large blue glowing bottle

'You got some on board!'

'Yes. Snatcher's mob have such contempt for boxtrolls we knew they wouldn't search him. Now open your mouth.'

Marjorie gave him a few drops of its contents on a spoon. 'It tastes like violets.'

As the taste spread over his tongue he felt a tingling in his body and the odd craving that had been occupying Arthur's mind seemed to just slip away.

'Now go and tell the others to get down here.'

Small groups of his friends disappeared below deck and returned looking happier.

As the last of the five sacks went in the boiler Kipper asked Snatcher what to do.

'Burn another sack! We need to go faster. And by the way, would it be just as quick to get to somewhere like Camembert in France as Ratbridge?'

'No, Camembert is inland.'

'Well, just get on with the stoking and head for England.'

'And when we finish that sack?'

'Burn some more! Just get us back to Ratbridge as fast as you can.'

Kipper smiled to himself. Snatcher had been given his own medicine and now didn't care if all the seeds got burnt.

'Stoke the boilers and full steam ahead!'

It took only a few more sacks until they were clear of the doldrums, but Snatcher ordered more seeds to be burnt. He and his mob were so infected with the fumes of the seeds

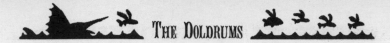

that cheese plagued their every waking moment. All that drove them now was the idea of cheese and the only place they could think that they could get hold of some was the woods around Ratbridge.

Fish moved to the stern deck with Kipper because Snatcher wanted to be closer to home and took the place on the bow.

Then as the last sack became empty they reached home waters.

Snatcher came aft and spoke. 'I want you to anchor off Weston-super-mare. It's a town down the coast from Bristol.'

'I know it,' said Kipper. 'My mum used to drag me there when I was a kid. Why do you want to stop there?'

'Never you mind. Just get us there.'

As the sun rose the following morning the anchor was dropped. They were about a mile from the coast but the water was very shallow.

Snatcher ordered his men to lock the crew below. 'We don't want any interference while we get on with me plan.'

Arthur and the others sat in their hammocks.

'What is he up to?'

'No good I'm sure but at least he's not got any seeds left.'

Then there was a bump and the ship became still.

'What's happened?'

'The tide must have gone out. We must be on the sand.'

There seemed to be a lot of activity above them and then

it went quiet. After a few more hours the ship seemed to be floating again but apart from the sound of water there was little other noise.

'What do we do now?'

'I think they have deserted us. It's probably the time to escape from here.'

'How do we do that?'

Fish took a crowbar from under his box and handed it to Kipper. Kipper pushed the end of it into the crack at the edge of the hatch and pushed.

There was a crack and the hatch popped open. Everyone rushed up on deck. Willbury was right. Snatcher and his men had gone . . . and so had all the bits of the monster.

Fish took a crowbar from under his box

'Attack of the seventy-foot monster! Read all about it!'

Chapter 13

BRISTOL

With Snatcher and his men out of the way, and a following wind, it only took a few hours for the ship to reach Bristol. A pilot came out to meet them and guide them back up the river. As they came to the dock they put in to buy some coal for the boiler as there was now almost nothing onboard left to burn. As they tied up Arthur heard a boy crying out:

'*Evening Post, Evening Post!* Read all about it. Attack of the seventy-foot monster! Read all about it!'

Arthur rushed down the gangplank, bought a paper, and started to read.

'SOMERSET VILLAGE ATTACKED BY HUGE MONSTER!

This afternoon word arrived that the village of Cheddar was attacked by a seventy-foot tall monster. The village is the last resting home of the cave-dwelling Cheddar cheeses, and these seemed to be the target. As the monster attacked and tried to gain entrance to the caves, the cheeses made off down the tunnels deep into the bowels of the earth. Denied its quarry, the monster made off in a north-easterly direction. Unconfirmed sightings of the monster were also made at Weston. Witnesses claim the monster emerged from the sea at low tide.'

Arthur finished reading and ran back onto the ship.

'Quick. Snatcher is on the rampage. We have to get back to Ratbridge.'

Quickly they cast off again and headed up river towards the canal. Tom and Bert took up position up in the crow's nest with the telescope and scanned the countryside for any signs of a monster.

Tom and Bert took up position up in the crow's nest

Arthur stood on the bow with Fish and, when they reached the canal, helped operate the lock gates. It was another half an hour before there was a cry from Bert.

'There she blows! Monster at twenty-five degrees to port.' They all looked out over the port bow.

Over the tops of some trees in the distance they saw the shape of the monster's head.

'It's heading for Ratbridge!' shouted Bert.

They saw the shape of the monster's head

'IT'S A BLOOMING MONSTER AND IT'S COMING THIS WAY!'

Chapter 14

CHEEZILLA!

The Ratbridge police now spent every afternoon patrolling the town walls and keeping an eye out for cheese-crazed inhabitants planning a break to satisfy their lust. If they'd only needed to guard the gates it would have been easy but now the cheese-crazed inhabitants had taken to using ropes and ladders to escape over the walls as the sun set in a desperate attempt to get to the woods to hunt the remaining cheeses.

Constable Grunt was brewing up tea for his patrol and emptying the last brew's tea leaves over the wall when he happened to look across to the wood. In the distance over the trees he could vaguely make out something moving.

'What do you reckon that is?' he asked a fellow officer.

'Not sure. Maybe . . .' His friend scratched his head and looked perplexed. 'I don't know.'

'It seems to be getting bigger.'

'Or closer?'

'What shall we do?'

'Eeeer . . . Blow your whistle?'

Grunt did as suggested and from along the wall the police came to see what was up. Soon they all stood watching the 'thing' moving through the trees.

Inside the wall those with the craving who were watching the police for a chance to escape from the town started to climb the unguarded parts of the wall. Ladders appeared and bodies could soon be seen mounting the wall and dropping ropes over the outside. But before anyone had managed to actually escape one of the policemen who had better sight than the others spoke.

'It's a blooming monster.'

'A what!'

'IT'S A BLOOMING MONSTER AND IT'S COMING THIS WAY!'

'My Gud! What about them what's guarding the swamp. It's nearly out of the woods and then it will be on them!'

'Everybody blow your whistle to warn them!'

As the monster broke from the woods the policemen surrounding the swamp heard the noise from the town walls and then turned to see the huge creature. They did what was natural and ran away screaming.

Across the town word travelled that there was something coming and people flocked to the walls to get a look. But as they crammed the walls they saw how huge and dangerous it looked and everybody started to scream.

The ship, fuelled with coal, made fast progress up the canal and was in clear sight of the town when the monster broke from the woods.

'Stop the engine!' Bert cried from the crow's nest.

Everyone aboard rushed to the rail to watch as the mighty beast began lurching towards the nearby swamp.

'What's he going to do now?' Kipper asked.

'Heaven knows, with Snatcher crazed with the cheese lust,' answered Willbury.

'I reckon he'll try to snap up any last remaining cheeses and then turn on the town,' said Bert.

'So what do we do?' asked Kipper. Everybody thought hard but it was Arthur that spoke first.

'Use his cheese lust,' suggested Arthur tentatively.

'What do you mean?' asked Kipper.

'Well, he wants cheese desperately and we need to slip him some of the antidote before he devours the last of the cheese or destroys the town while he's crazed. Can't we combine the two?'

'But how?'

'Make a fake cheese filled with the antidote.'

Kipper smiled. 'I get it. We bamboozle him with a cheese. But how do we get it in front of him?'

'Cheeses have legs don't they? One of us is inside the cheese,' offered Arthur.

'But wouldn't that be putting whoever is inside the cheese in terrible danger?'

'We make sure they have an escape,' Arthur replied. 'And choose the fastest runner to be the cheese.'

'But how do we make a cheese?'

Arthur looked thoughtful. 'For the smell socks might work. Have you never noticed the pong that dirty ones make?'

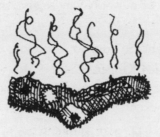

'For the smell socks might work'

'And boy do we ever have some dirty socks,' said Kipper enthusiastically.

'I reckon I could mould a cheesy body with sock smell and the antidote pretty easily in the galley,' Bert offered.

'Well then. It might just work,' chuckled Tom.

'Great. But who's the fastest runner?' asked Marjorie.

'Us rats are pretty fast,' Tom boasted.

'Not that fast really. Your legs are pretty short. I think in an open space a human could run faster,' replied Kipper.

'I'll do it,' said Arthur. 'I can run fast and it was my idea.'

Willbury looked very concerned. 'It is too dangerous. There is a real danger of being eaten. Besides, your legs are not that long.'

'And imagine what the smell would be like,' added Bert. 'It might make you pass out.'

'Anybody got a better idea?' asked Arthur.

No one had.

Arthur looked about. 'Well then, we have to do something and fast. It may be our only way to save the real cheeses and Ratbridge.'

'Arthur is right. So how do we choose who is going to be our cheese?' asked Kipper.

'A race. We could have a race up the deck,' suggested Bert.

Willbury looked at Arthur. 'I really don't want you involved in this.'

Arthur smiled back. 'This is about who is fastest and can do the job best. It has to be the fastest runner. Anyway, I think you need to give me a chance to be useful. Remember that you didn't want me to come on this voyage at all. Where would you all be now if I hadn't stowed away?'

'That's true. But hopefully you won't win.'

'A race from one end of the deck to the other it is then,' said Bert.

Even though it was going to be a very dangerous mission, everyone crowded to the fore end of the deck and Willbury set them off with a count of three.

By the time Arthur had reached halfway along the deck Fish was in the lead, just a few paces ahead.

'I know I can do this,' Arthur thought to himself as he pushed himself as hard as he could and began to catch up with the boxtroll.

Fish was in the lead

He gritted his teeth and pumped his legs as hard as he could, then as the side of the ship came closer he reached out with his hand and stretched.

'ARTHUR'S WON!'

His friends crowded around him. They looked pleased for him—but very concerned too.

'Well done! But I'll go if you don't want to,' offered Kipper.

'I think that would be best,' said Willbury—but then he bowed his head in resignation as Arthur looked him in the eye and spoke very firmly.

'I am the fastest and I think that I can do the job. Let's get ready. Time to make our cheese substitute!'

Bert quickly took charge of making the 'cheese'. First he got everybody to put every dirty sock they could find in the biggest saucepan they had. He added water, then after a good stir he strained off the liquid into another pan and added flour and some yellow ointment that they used to rub on scuffed knees.

'And of course our secret ingredient!'

Fish reached inside his box and pulled out the glowing blue bottle. Bert took it and tipped its contents into the mixture. After a bit of a stir it became much thicker and looked like bright yellow dough.

Bert took it and tipped its contents into the mixture

'Still a bit soggy. How are we going to get it to stick to Arthur?'

'I have some glue that goes hard after ten minutes. We could mix that in?' suggested Marjorie.

'Very well. We'll use that. If we cut two holes in the bottom of a barrel we can put Arthur's legs through them and use it as a mould. Arthur, strip down to your underpants, then we will cover you in grease.'

While Marjorie fetched the quick setting glue, Arthur was readied and two holes were cut in the bottom of a barrel.

Then Arthur was lowered into the barrel, leaving him with his legs sticking out of the bottom and his head out of the top.

The reality of the situation began to dawn on Arthur. Yes, he had won the race, but would he really be fast enough to outrun the monster? Maybe Willbury was right—maybe he really *would* get eaten . . . But it was too late for doubts now.

'Are you ready?' Bert asked.

'Ready as I'll ever be.'

The glue was tipped into the dough mixture and stirred in.

'You'd better be quick or it will go hard in the pan.'

'OK!'

The foul-smelling mixture was tipped into the barrel around Arthur

The foul-smelling mixture was tipped into the barrel around Arthur. It felt warm around his belly as the mixture hardened. After a couple of minutes the mixture stiffened and Bert declared it ready.

'Take the barrel apart!' Bert instructed and the metal hoops were knocked loose and slid off. The barrel fell apart leaving Arthur standing on the deck looking like . . . an enormous cheese.

Arthur looking like an enormous cheese

'Perfect! Not only does he look like a cheese but he also smells like one.'

Arthur's arms were free above his new cheese body so he was able to hold his nose.

'So what happens now?' asked Willbury in a worried tone.

'Arthur lures the monster away from the real cheeses in the woods,' replied Bert

'But where to?' Willbury seemed increasingly worried.

'If we dig a hole in the ground I could slip out of the costume into it,' suggested Arthur.

'I guess we need to dig the hole then?' said Kipper.

'Where?' Willbury was starting to panic. 'This really is not a good idea.'

'Don't worry. Somewhere between the woods and the town so he doesn't have to run too far,' answered Kipper. 'Our Arthur can do it!'

The sound of roaring rang out from the woods.

'We'd better be quick! Grab a spade, Tom, and come with me,' shouted Kipper.

The pirates jumped over the side and ran to a place not far from the town wall. There they quickly dug a hole a little taller than Arthur and just wide enough for his body.

They quickly dug a hole

Arthur watched from the deck of the ship. He had been wrapped in oilskin to stop the smell getting out too early. They didn't want anything to happen before they were ready.

Bert and Fish stood next to him.

'What do you think I should do to attract them?'

'I think you won't have to worry too much. And we'll

help. You'll just have to run about a bit like a cheese until they get close.'

Kipper and Tom returned.

'Are you ready?'

'Yes,' said a nervous Arthur.

'You don't have to do this! You can still back out.' Willbury was looking very pale and Marjorie led him away from the crowd.

Arthur looked about for a moment, with a worried expression on his face. Kipper put a hand on his shoulder.

'He's right. You don't have to do this.'

'No. I want to do it.'

'Good lad!'

The gangplank was lowered to the canal bank, and Arthur smiled at Kipper and his friends. 'Well, let's go then!'

'Are you ready?'

Arthur stood waiting a few yards from the hole

Chapter 15

A CHEESY ENDING

Arthur stood waiting a few yards from the hole. It seemed pointless and a bit embarrassing to start running about before anybody saw him, so he waited for the others to do their work.

Half the crew went into the town. The other half headed towards the monster.

Then it began.

'Cheese! Cheese! A huge wild cheese!' All over town the cry rang out. Heads popped out of windows.

Heads popped out of windows

'Where's the cheese? Where's the cheese?'

'Just outside the town wall. It's huge!'

The pirates' cries were soon mixed with the sound of running footsteps.

Across the fields the rest of the crew were in sight of the monster.

'Cheese! Cheese! Cheese!' they shouted as they waved their arms to get noticed.

Inside the head of the monster Snatcher's ears heard the cry.

'Who's shouting that?'

'I don't know but it's coming from outside.'

'It must be a trap. Why else would anybody be shouting cheese?'

The eyes of the monsters turned to the shouting crew, who then pointed towards a small shape just outside the town walls. The monster looked up and saw the shape.

'It looks like a cheese, boss!'

The nose then reported back. 'I can smell it. Ripe smelly cheese.'

'Don't seem quite right. Hold on, boys!'

The thought of cheese was too much for his mob. No way were they going to hang about if there was a chance of eating cheese.

'Legs full ahead! Let's get some cheese,' screamed Gristle.

'No! NO!' shouted Snatcher. 'It's probably a trap.' But even he was salivating.

Arthur was getting worried as he saw the monster turn towards him. He spun round towards the town and was about to start running in that direction when a mob started to pour from the town gate.

'CHEESE! CHEESE! IT'S A CHEESE!'

He was not sure which way to turn.

'Stay calm! I have to stay calm . . . and act like a cheese.'

He decided to run in circles around the hole. If he did that he could get to it at any moment.

He decided to run in circles around the hole

The monster and the mob grew closer. Arthur thought it looked as if the monster would reach him first. He was not sure this was a good thing. It might scare off the mob, so he stopped and waggled his cheese body at the mob.

The cries of 'CHEESE' grew louder.

Arthur turned to check and was horrified. Powered by the lust for cheese the monster was striding rapidly towards him, much faster than he had imagined. It was almost time to run . . . NO! He mustn't run. He just had to jump in the hole.

The urge to turn and run was huge but he resisted it. So he stood right over the hole with one leg either side.

'Please let the jaws not miss me . . .'

The monster was striding rapidly towards him

The monster was now only yards from him.

Even Snatcher was caught up in the frenzy and was screaming commands. 'We have to get the cheese before those others get it! Open the jaws, drop the head, and CHOMP!'

Arthur watched as the monster lunged for him.

'Time for the hole!'

He breathed out, brought his legs together and put his arms straight up in the air. Arthur felt the cheese loosen around him as he dropped, then the bottom of the cheese hit the ground around the edge of the hole. There was a jerk as he fell free and continued down.

The jaws snapped down on the cheese. In the approaching mob, the cheese-lust turned to rage. 'It's got our cheese!'

'Get it before it swallows!'

The cheese-crazed mob fell upon the monster and started to tear it apart. Driven wild with desire they were fearless.

Snatcher and his crew knew that the fight was on. It was every man for himself.

Arthur's friends watched the mayhem with anxiety, uncertain exactly what was happening.

'Let us pray he managed to drop into the hole. I should never have allowed this,' Willbury said in horror.

The others kept quiet and most of them had their fingers crossed behind their backs.

It looked as if Arthur would be very lucky to survive. The mob were crawling over the monster like ants. Bits of the huge creature were torn away in the struggle. Then the 'cheese' appeared, held above the heads of the mob and the fighting grew more intense as figures jumped from the carcass of the wrecked monster to try to get to the cheese.

The mob were crawling over the monster like ants

'I can't bear to watch,' Willbury muttered as he turned away. The others strained their eyes in the hope of getting a glimpse of an un-injured Arthur.

It was becoming a vicious battle and in the melee the cheese hit the ground and shattered into a thousand pieces. The mob screamed and fell upon the fragments, kicking and fighting for every crumb.

'They look like a herd of starved pigs,' said a very worried Tom.

'Let's just hope they only eat the cheese,' replied Kipper.

As they watched the mob seemed to slow as it searched for the last tiny fragments. Then an eerie calm settled on the whole scene.

'We'd better go and rescue Arthur,' cried Kipper. This triggered a rush from the ship as Arthur's friends headed towards the hole, where they hoped he was still hidden.

As they got closer they had to push past the cheese maniacs to get to the hole.

Fish reached it first and looked down into the darkness. All he could see was mud and earth. Then the mud moved and a head emerged and blinked.

'Hello, Fish!'

'I missed you so much!'

Chapter 16

THE WIND-UP . . .

The friends all let out their breath with relief that Arthur was all right. Then smiles crossed their faces.

'Thank heavens!' intoned Willbury.

Kipper joined Fish in pulling Arthur from the hole and what emerged was a very muddy and worried looking hero. Arthur looked about frantically. He saw what he was looking for near the edge of the now quiet mob.

'Grandfather!'

His grandfather looked rather blankly back at him. 'Arthur?'

Arthur ran to him and hugged him. 'I missed you so much. How do you feel? Are you all right?'

Grandfather thought for a moment. 'I'm not sure. Where am I?'

All around them the once crazed mob were sitting around looking bewildered.

Marjorie watched and then spoke. 'I think the antidote has taken effect. But it has left them a bit bamboozled.'

The mania was gone.

Then Bert sprang to life. 'We have to round up Snatcher and his mob. Let's be quick before they get their wits back.'

The pirates and rats quickly gathered up Snatcher and his men from amid the monster's wreckage and the confused huddles of now-cured cheese fiends, and tied them up.

Willbury watched as Snatcher was secured by Kipper and Tom.

Snatcher was secured by Kipper and Tom

'Look in his pockets. He might have those contracts we signed.'

Snatcher was in no state to protest, and Kipper searched him.

'Is this what you want?' he said pulling out a large wad of papers.

Willbury took them and flicked through them. 'Yes. I think it's getting cold. Shall we light a fire?'

Just as the ashes of the papers were being rubbed into the grass the Squeakers arrived.

'Right then. What's going on here?'

'These are the men that are behind the awful cheese mania that has been plaguing the town,' Willbury replied. Then he turned to where the doctor was standing amongst the crowd, not as yet tied up. 'And this "doctor" will explain everything. You might also like to contact the Edinburgh police and enquire about unsolved hair shaving crimes. I think you'll find he was very involved.'

The police had not had much luck recently and as they were paid by the number of arrests they made, they were very happy to have Snatcher, all his crew, and the doctor.

As the prisoners were led away to be locked up they began to recover and as they did it dawned on them how bad a predicament they were in. They were not happy and even though he was at the heart of it Snatcher took every opportunity when the police had not got their eyes on him to kick any of his men that got within reach.

'I don't think with all the trouble they've caused the town that they are going to escape justice this time,' Willbury observed to Marjorie. They both smiled.

Meanwhile the still recovering cheese maniacs wandered back home somewhat dazed and confused. This just left

Arthur and all his friends amongst the broken wreckage of the monster.

'I think we've all done rather well. Would anybody like to come back to the shop for a celebratory bucket of cocoa?' Willbury offered. 'I at least could do with a sit down.'

Arthur took his grandfather's hand and led him home. As they walked Grandfather slowly regained his old self, but fortunately not his old ills. Arthur told him of their adventures.

'Seems to me that you can take care of yourself,' said Grandfather.

Willbury, who had been quietly walking alongside, looked rather bashful and spoke. 'It's not just himself he can look after. I don't think any of us would have managed without him.'

'Thank you,' Arthur smiled. 'I did say I could be useful!'

'I did I say I could be useful!'

Willbury just smiled back.

The shop became so full with Arthur and all his friends, that some had to sit on the stairs.

Upstairs in Arthur's bedroom sat a small group. The other boxtrolls and Titus were welcoming back their old friend Fish. Long into the night they asked him questions about the voyage and as he told them they shook their heads in wonder.

Long into the night they asked him questions about the voyage

Below them in the shop the party got a little wild. Bucket after bucket of cocoa was passed around, until they could take no more, but still everybody talked about their adventures.

Arthur sat by the fire close to Grandfather and they listened to the others.

'I wish I could have been there with you. I would have loved to have seen that island and the southern seas.'

Arthur smiled. He felt lucky, despite all the troubles they had.

'Next time!'

'I hope that is not going to be for a few weeks,' said Willbury. 'Unlike you, I need to recover.'

Willbury then stood and held up one of the almost empty buckets of cocoa.

'To Arthur. The finest, most courageous cheese there ever was.'

'ARTHUR!' shouted his friends.

'Next time!'

Join Arthur and his friends in the first wonderfully weird Ratbridge Chronicles adventure, HERE BE MONSTERS!

Book 1	Book 2	Book 3

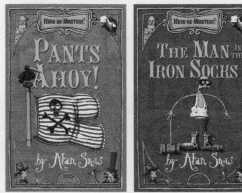

ISBN 978-0-19-275540-7 ISBN 978-0-19-275541-4 ISBN 978-0-19-275542-1

Beneath the streets of Ratbridge, something is stirring ... It is up to Arthur, prevented from going home by the evil Snatcher, to save the day. With the help of Willbury Nibble QC (retired), a band of boxtrolls, some cabbageheads, and Marjorie the inventor, can Arthur keep Ratbridge from danger—and find his way home?

Alan Snow is a well-known author and illustrator of children's books, and has also worked in many fields of design and animation.

WORSE THINGS HAPPEN AT SEA! is his second story set in the wonderfully weird world of Ratbridge, and follows HERE BE MONSTERS!

www.ratbridgechronicles.com

Come in and explore the wonderful world of
Ratbridge at our RATBRIDGE CHRONICLES! website.
You'll find all sorts of bits and bobs to keep you as
happy as a boxtroll in a pile of nuts and bolts.

Look out for competitions, games,
screensavers, maps, and much, much more!

www.ratbridgechronicles.com